The Vampire in My Basement

KC De La Rosa

Contents

Letter from the Author

Hello!

I'd just like to thank you for picking up The Vampire in My Basement, my monster romance debut novella! This story is quite possibly the most self indulgent thing I've ever written, and I hope that you love reading it as much as I loved writing it. Haley and Vasile were so much fun to write (and so was Brenda—but you'll meet her soon!)

As always, I want my readers to protect themselves while reading. So here are some content warnings for The Vampire in My Basement:

- Blood (in the vampire kind of way)

- Biting (also, in the vampire kind of way)

- Recreational drug use (weed gummies)

- Internalized transphobia, very briefly mentioned

- Needles used for injecting medication (in epilogue)

Please take care while reading. I hope you enjoy your time with Haley and Vasile!

KC

Dedication

For anyone who has daydreamed about being a vampire's personal juice box.

And for the trans mascs who couldn't tell if they wanted Edward Cullen or wanted to *be* him. Sometimes it's both.

Chapter One

Haley Christine Anderson had a house with a fucking fireplace and hardwood floors. Not even those fake hardwood floors that were actually cheap laminate flooring on top of an even cheaper wooden foundation. This was real wood, baby.

She laid out on the floor in front of her fireplace–she'd have to get wood for it later–and tapped the screen of her phone. Getting some furniture might be a good idea, but she'd drained the last of her bank account on getting herself and her car over here. New York was no short distance from her hometown of Atlanta, Georgia, and her truck was a hell of a gas guzzler. She hadn't really *needed* the truck in Atlanta. Some weird part of her just liked taking up more space than she was privy to. But out here in New York, her truck wasn't anywhere near the biggest on the road anymore.

She typed 'furniture store near me' into the search engine on her phone and scrolled through them, looking for the one that sounded the cheapest. A chirp sounded from beside her, followed by the brush of a tiny body of feathers against her arm. "What happen?" Brenda asked, the tiny blue parakeet hopping onto her shoulder.

"What do you think, Bren? Do you think 'Discount Furniture' is cheaper than 'Furniture For Less'? For less than *what?*" Haley pursed her lips and Brenda tapped her clawed feet.

Brenda let out a string of squawked 'what's, and Haley huffed. "Well, *that's* helpful." She was just starting to scroll again when Rhea's face popped onto her screen, followed by a particularly aggressive vibrate of her phone. She jumped, dropping her phone directly onto her face. Brenda squeaked, flapping her wings in protest and abandoning Haley on the floor with nothing but her shame and a sore nose.

"I think you just broke my nose," she groaned, jabbing the speaker button and shoving herself to her slippered feet. She was *not* going to ruin this beautiful hardwood by wearing her shoes on it.

"I'm not responsible for you dropping your phone on your face," Rhea shot back, and Haley hated how well she knew her. She shuffled into her empty dining room, trailing her fingers along the island counter, complete with a cute little window into the kitchen. All she had to do was buy some bar stools.

"*And* you scared Brenda away. She's pissed." Brenda let out a caw of assent from her perch atop the fridge.

"Fuck off, Brenda," Rhea shouted, her voice crackling through the line.

"Fuck off!" Brenda repeated, chanting the phrase to herself as she flew through the dinette window and back to her cage, the one piece of furniture Haley had bothered to bring. She'd hoped that, one day, Rhea and Brenda would be friends, but they seemed pretty dead-set on antagonizing each other every time they interacted. Haley had tried to point out to Rhea that Brenda was just copying *her,* but Rhea wouldn't hear it. Like any rational adult, she decided instead to have a vendetta against a parakeet.

"So," Rhea said, dragging out the 'o' in the word, "how's the new place? Is it just as cute as it was in pictures?"

Haley didn't want to gloat... but Rhea had opened herself up for it. "Oh my God, Ray, it's even cuter than I thought. There's a little window between the dining room and the kitchen, and the kitchen has *real marble counters.* Even the *fridge* is fancy. It has an option for crushed or cubed ice!"

"Wow, look at you with ice. You're really movin' up in the world."

"I know, right!" Haley laughed, exiting the opposite side of the kitchen and into the hallway. She opened one of the doors to a beige carpeted bedroom, which she didn't entirely love. And that was precisely why this room was relegated to the position of guest bedroom. "I gotta get a bed for your room. I'll even let you pick it, since you're probably the only person who's ever gonna stay in here."

"Aww, thanks. You think a California King can fit in there?"

Haley did a quick visual scan of the room. "Nope."

"Dammit. Fine, I'll settle with a regular king. Or a queen if I *really* have to."

Haley shut the door and opened the next door down. *Her* bedroom. Honestly, this was what had sold her on the house in the first place. It faced south, meaning it faced out of the neighborhood towards the trees that she knew would look like something out of a painting once winter came and coated them in snow. The window jutted out from the house, the ledge big enough for Haley to sit on. And she had every intention of making it comfy with entirely too many pillows.

"You'll go down to a queen? Ugh, we love a woman of the people. Turns out celebrities are just like us."

"I'm a humble woman, Haley. I won't let my fame go to my head," Rhea said. "Just don't tell my fifty thousand Switch followers that I'm sleeping on a *queen* bed instead of a king."

"God forbid. I know *I* couldn't take video gaming advice from a lowly queen bed sleeper." Haley peered into her closet–spacious, but not *too* spacious–and realized she should probably start hanging things up. Maybe this house would be the driving force to make her actually hang her clothes up instead of digging them out of the clean clothes pile on her desk chair as she needed them.

She left her room and stood in the doorway for a second. She *really* should have at least gotten a couch delivered or something. Her feet carried her back to the living room, where Brenda preened her feathers in her cage. Even her *bird* had more furniture than she did. All she'd brought for herself was her clothes and her embarrassingly large collection of smutty monster books.

She *did* have a desk and a chair that weren't yet assembled, sitting in boxes in the corner of the living room. Assembling them was a task she really wasn't prepared for. Normally, Rhea built all of her furniture. Haley could never entirely wrap her head around the instructions. She'd inevitably end up screwing something into the wrong piece, getting pissed off, and giving up until the next day, or until Rhea could come over and put it together in approximately ten minutes.

The laundry room was right next to the entrance to the garage—yet another thing that made her feel stupid rich—and right next to that was a door she didn't remember seeing before. The doorknobs of all the other doors were shiny and gold, probably just replaced. But this one was painted over with the same ugly, stark white that the other doors were painted.

"Would you be suspicious of a door with a painted-over handle?" Haley asked, testing the doorknob with her free hand. It turned, but the door didn't budge when Haley gave it a hefty shove.

"Uh, yeah. Probably," Rhea said. "Please don't tell me you have one of those."

"Okay, I don't." Haley squared her shoulders and shoved her shoulder into the door, but it still didn't give. "And that door is definitely *not* locked."

"Oh, dude, what the fuck." Haley could practically hear the nose wrinkle in her voice. "Nope. Move out. As a matter of fact, burn the house down. There is absolutely a skeleton or a ghost or a zombie down there."

Well... Haley could handle a skeleton or a ghost or a zombie. She'd rather *not* handle a zombie, but at least she was pretty sure she could take one in a fight. "Well now I wanna know which one of those it is!"

"If I ever get trapped in a scary movie, I'm sacrificing you because I know your stupid ass would get killed first anyway," Rhea said. "Seriously, Haley, that sounds dangerous."

How dangerous could it be, really? It was a room in a house in the middle of Ithaca, New York. The scariest thing here was the horde of zombie nurses swarming the Dunkin at seven a.m. after an overnight shift at the hospital.

Maybe there was a zombie nurse in her basement. "I'm gonna try and shove it open again," she said, and rammed her shoulder into the door one last time before Rhea could protest. It creaked under her weight at the second shove, and upon the third, the door swung open, nearly sending Haley barreling down the unlit stairs.

"Holy shit, I did it," she breathed, and Rhea screeched from the other end of the phone.

"Okay, you *better* stay on the phone with me and tell me what you find down there. I won't hesitate to call the cops on your landlord if you find something weird," Rhea threatened, and Haley had no reason not to believe her. Hell, she wouldn't be surprised if Rhea came up here herself to threaten her landlord with the exact same thing.

Haley felt around on the wall for a light switch and flicked it up, but was greeted only by the sizzle of a dead bulb. "Oh, cool. Lightbulb's out." She swiped up on her screen and turned on the flashlight of her phone, the splintered wooden steps beneath her bathed in a beam of white light.

She crept down the stairs slowly, as not to startle whatever spectre had taken up residence in her house. "So far, so good," Haley whispered. Her slippers found the bottom of the stairs; the floor of the basement was concrete that didn't look like it had been swept in years. She shone her light around the room.

Empty. Haley snorted. "Okay, wow. What a waste of time. There's not shit down here."

"No way. There has to be something." Rhea hummed. "No doors?"

Haley waved the beam of her flashlight over the blank walls and nearly missed the door on the wall opposite the stairs. It was painted the same depressing shade of white as her doors upstairs, as the walls down here. "Oh, yeah, there *is* a door."

"Just a door? Nothing else?" She could practically hear the wrinkle in Rhea's nose. "I don't know... I don't love the sound of that."

Yeah, it was a little creepy. But Haley had come this far—backing out now would be a waste. She crossed the floor and turned the knob to the door.

This one wasn't locked. It gave way easily, opening in front of her. "Okay, walking in," Haley announced. She took a few timid steps before shining her light around the room.

The room was only *mostly* empty. The only thing it held was a tall, rectangular box, propped up against one of the walls. "What the hell?" Haley whispered, approaching it slowly.

"What? What is it?" Rhea demanded, her own voice dropped to a whisper, too.

"It's... a weird, long box," Haley said, shining her light around it once she was close enough to see the details. The box was made of proper wood rather than cardboard, which Haley thought was strange. "It's taller than *me.*"

"There's a mummy in there," Rhea said with a confidence Haley didn't think she deserved to have. "That's *definitely* mummy territory, Hales. You're gonna open that thing and it's gonna put a curse on your entire bloodline."

Well, it was a good thing Haley didn't want kids. "Should I open it?" she whispered.

"No! Don't you dare!"

Haley's light moved along the seam of the box until she found a hinge. *Bingo.* She dug her nails into the small crack in the opposite side of the box and swung it open, the lid slamming against the wall with a solid *crack.*

And then Haley screamed.

Chapter Two

"What? What did you see?" Rhea demanded from the other end of the phone.

There was a dead guy in a box in her basement. A dead guy who didn't show many signs of being dead aside from the sickly pallor of his skin and the fact that she was pretty sure he wasn't breathing. She stuck her finger under his nose. Yep. Not breathing.

He had to be freshly dead, because his corpse wasn't bloated. She didn't dare touch him to see if rigor mortis had set in yet. "I think this guy is dead," she whispered, her throat tightening.

Haley's mind raced with possibilities. There didn't appear to be signs of a struggle. His skin was perfect, almost infuriatingly so. The only parts of it she could see were his face, neck, and hands. The rest of him was covered by the deep red waistcoat he wore atop a frilly undershirt, a pair of tight black pants, and what looked like riding boots.

"Dead?" Rhea squeaked. "Oh my God. I'm calling the cops right now."

"Wait a minute." The last thing Haley wanted to deal with right now was the police. "It's the middle of the day. He's in a box that kind of looks like a coffin. What if he's a vampire?"

The line went silent for a moment and Haley thought Rhea had hung up. "Are you high?"

Well, yeah. "A little. I took an edible just before I came into the house–"

"Jesus Christ, why did I ever think you could survive out there on your own? You find a dead body in your house and you think it's a *vampire*?" Rhea clicked her tongue, and Haley could practically feel the judgmental stare. "Vampires don't exist, Haley."

"They're very secretive, y'know." Haley looked over him again. He was... handsome, really, with high, prominent cheekbones, a long, round jaw and plump, though pale, lips. His hair was curly and, from what Haley could see, quite long. It appeared to tie back behind his head at the nape of his neck, a few loose curls framing his face.

There had to be some kind of proof of who he was around here. "I gotta replace this lightbulb," she muttered under her breath, shining her flashlight around the room.

"No, you need to *leave it alone,*" Rhea said, and Haley had half a mind to hang up on her. What fun was a best friend who didn't help you indulge in your delusions? "Just go upstairs. Don't rummage around in his pockets, don't look for *anything–*"

Rummaging around in his pockets! Why hadn't Haley thought of that? "You're a genius," she said, plopping her phone on top of the box to shove her hands into his pockets. One of them was empty, save for an inordinate amount of lint, but her hand found a piece of folded paper in the other. *Maybe* it was paper. It was brittle and dry, folded up into a tidy square.

"Did you not hear the *don't* part of that sentence?" Rhea demanded from on top of the box.

She did not. She reached for her phone and shone the flashlight onto the paper. The text was in a language Haley didn't understand. "God, this has to be *hundreds* of years old," she said, laying it flat on her hand as carefully as she could. "I swear, this man is a vampire."

"My asking questions does *not* make me complicit in this," Rhea said, "but what did you find?"

"It looks like an official paper of some kind. There's a seal on it... but I don't know what language this is."

Rhea let out a long, resigned sigh. "Take a picture of it and I'll see if I recognize it. Just keep it out of direct sunlight as much as you can."

Sounded like the words of a woman who was *very much* complicit in this. "Alright, alright. I'm gonna go upstairs to take the picture, if that makes you feel any better."

"It does. Thank you."

Haley closed the lid of the box and went back up the stairs, settling on the floor of the living room and taking a picture of the document before sending it to Rhea. In the light, it looked even older than it had downstairs. The parchment was frayed at the folds, a square of it threatening to fall off.

"This is a Cyrillic alphabet," Rhea said. If there was any sure-fire way to get her best friend roped into anything, it was to give her a chance to flex her history muscles. "And judging by how old this thing looks... I dunno, dude. This could be Russ-ian, Moldovan, Romanian–"

"Romanian?" She was right. She *had* to be. "Romania used to be Transylvania."

"No, Transylvania is *part* of what we now call Romania. It still exists." Rhea hummed in thought. "Okay, yeah. I'm googling it and this *does* look like the old Romanian Cyrillic alphabet."

Haley pumped her fist in the air. "He's a vam-pire! I knew it!" She hopped up, scooping the battered parchment into her hands. "Oh my God, my house came with a vampire. Shit, do you think he has squatter's rights?"

"You can't get squatter's rights in a house that someone *else* owns. This is *your* house!" Rhea groaned. "I gotta go. I have to get ready for work. But please, I'm begging you, for the sake of my sanity, don't do anything stupid."

That was a promise Haley would never be able to keep. "Sure, sure. Tell Camille I said hi." Camille was Rhea's boss, Haley's former boss, at the restaurant they'd met at ten years ago. And also Haley's ex. This was the one time Haley wished she'd listened to Rhea's advice—as it turned out, dating coworkers *was* a bad idea.

"I will not be doing that. Byeee!" Rhea hung up, leaving Haley to her own devices with nothing but a hunger for knowledge and maybe just a little bit of actual hunger. The munchies were starting to set in.

But she had to get to the bottom of this first. She scanned her phone's app store for a translation app and downloaded the first one she saw. It struggled with the outdated alphabet, but she managed to piece together snippets.

One word in the title was 'entry,' and then a date–April 21, 1798. Haley chewed her thumbnail thoughtfully, as if it might give her the answers, as she read over the rest of the sloppily translated text. Something about 'purpose for entering,' and then the word 'medicine.'

He could have been a doctor. He looked like a doctor. Or maybe he was coming to America to *obtain* some type of medicine? The rest of the document was so poorly translated, Haley couldn't glean anything further from it.

"Okay. So this guy is either *from* the 1700s, or he's just... really into history?" Haley said aloud to no one in particular.

But Brenda took it as an address to her, and she chirped in response. "Pretty bird?" she asked.

"Well, he *is* pretty, but not exactly a bird." She held the fragile paper as carefully as she could in the flat of her hand. She had to get to the bottom of this.

But before that, she needed a snack and a lightbulb for the basement. After a trip to retrieve a lightbulb and a burrito that she practically inhaled on her drive home, she felt ready to blow this case wide open. She finished the last of her edible gummy and went to work.

She switched out the lightbulb and turned it on, bathing the basement in light. It was just as empty as she expected it to be, with a few more spiderwebs than she saw the first time around. That was fine, she could handle a few spiderwebs.

She changed the lightbulb in the box's room, too, only to find it just as empty as the main floor. The box sat menacingly in the corner of the room, staring at her, daring her to solve its mystery.

And dammit, she was going to. She opened the lid again, more carefully this time, and came face to face once again with its occupant. He hadn't moved an inch.

This time, she dared to move his arm. It wasn't stiff in the slightest, but she could feel the cold radiating from him through his coat. She took one of his hands in hers and turned it over. His hand was small, elegant, with long-nailed fingers and a smattering of tiny scars.

"Vampires *are* real, right? I'm not going crazy?" she asked herself aloud. Or maybe she'd just taken one too many edibles. That was entirely likely.

But the edibles weren't making her see something that wasn't here. This guy, whoever he was, *was* here.

And there was a reason she was here, too. She slipped her hand under his coat to reach into his pants pockets, which also came up empty. Something about that made her chest ache. This guy was in a house completely alone, dead to the world, with nothing on him but a piece of paper. If anyone had come looking for him, they hadn't gone to much of an effort. The door to the basement had to have been locked like that for a *long* time.

"Who *are* you?" she asked him, opening up his piece of paper again as if she might be able to make sense of it under this new light. The words seemed to burn into her retinas now, and if anything, they made *less* sense now.

She folded the parchment back up, catching the pad of her finger on the edge of it. "Shit," she gasped, wringing her hand as the stinging immediately set in. "Thanks a lot. You gave me a papercut." She tucked the parchment back into his pocket and pulled her finger to her face to inspect it.

A pinprick of blood bubbled to the surface, and she went to pop it in her mouth to soothe it but stopped herself. Surely a vampire couldn't resist the siren song of fresh blood. She wafted her finger under his nose, but he didn't stir.

Either she was completely wrong about this whole thing or her blood just didn't smell good. And frankly, she didn't know which one was worse. Maybe she *did* need to call the cops and she was just impeding on a crime scene.

Haley closed the lid to the box and started toward the stairs. She was only just out of the room when a deafening crack sounded from the room behind her. She turned, and the last thing she saw before her back struck the hard concrete was a flash of red hurtling right for her.

Chapter Three

Teeth gnashed right before Haley's eyes, and she shoved the heel of her palm into the face of her attacker. "Get off me!" she shrieked.

Which, surprisingly, worked. The body on top of her fell to the side, clutching his head and groaning. "Your voice is like that of a banshee," he said, rubbing at his temples with his fingertips. "Must you *shriek* at me?" Much to her delight, his voice was sharpened by a Romanian accent.

Haley scoffed. It seemed that men from olden times came with all the audacity today's men had.

"Dude, you're the one who attacked *me*. What else would you expect me to do other than *shriek*?"

The man blinked and then stared at Haley, giving her a look into his blood-red eyes. She hadn't noticed the bags tugging at the skin beneath his eyes before. He kind of looked like shit, but she couldn't imagine she'd look much better after being asleep for two hundred years.

God, she couldn't wait to rub this in Rhea's face.

He cleared his throat, straightening the ruffles at his throat. "Ah... my apologies. I appear to have lost myself. I indulged in a touch of laudanum last night, and–" He stopped, his eyes raking over Haley in a way that seemed more apprehensive than anything. He made a big show of averting his gaze, shielding his eyes with both hands. "I did not intend to gaze upon you in such a state of undress."

Undress? Haley looked down at her checkered sleep shorts and oversized band tee she'd gotten from a concert years ago. Well, okay, maybe she wasn't the *most* presentable. "Uh, it's okay. You can look, I don't care."

The man shook his head vehemently, only to clutch his head and whine with pain afterwards. God, he was pathetic, but in a weirdly charming way. "No, no, it is improper. Actually, I should just be on my way. I have patients to tend to." He shoved himself to his feet and wobbled. Haley jumped to her feet, clutching his arm and steadying him.

This seemed to catch his attention. His gaze caught hers, and her heart stuttered. "Okay, as much as I *really* don't wanna be the one to tell you this... the world out there probably isn't what you're expecting it to be."

He eyed her warily, tugging his arm from her grip. "I have been in America long enough to know what I am in for," he said, blinking a few more times to orient himself.

This wasn't gonna be easy. Haley whistled. "What year do you think we're in right now?"

"1809," he said, as if it were the most obvious thing in the world.

Suck it, Rhea. Haley clamped a hand on his shoulder, another move he seemed affronted by. "It's 2026, buddy."

The man scoffed, once again shrugging her off. "I may have consumed a *lot* of laudanum last night, but not *that* much. You cannot fool me."

Haley pointed above them to the bare lightbulb hanging from its fixture. "You ever seen one of those before?"

He followed her finger, staring directly into the lightbulb's beam and let out what Haley could only assume was a curse in Romanian. "What devilish thing is this?" He reached out to touch it, and Haley battled the urge to let him before gently guiding his hand away.

"A lightbulb. It was invented in, like, the 1800s."

He looked away from it finally, squinting his eyes in what was probably hangover light sensitivity. "Fascinating."

"Just you wait 'til you see a television," Haley snorted. Maybe she shouldn't throw too much at him at once. "So you've been... asleep? Since 1809?"

The man looked straight forward, his gaze unfocused on the concrete wall ahead of them. "It appears that way." A look crossed his face that Haley couldn't quite place. "I did not anticipate the laudanum having quite that much of an effect on me."

Haley didn't know what laudanum was, but she could tell this poor man was in the throes of a wicked hangover. "Yeah. Classic laudanum." She leaned back against the wall, folding her arms over her chest. "What's your name?"

"Dr. Vasile Albescu." Ooh, *doctor*. The name rolled off his tongue, soft and elegant, and it made Haley almost embarrassed to share her own.

"I'm Haley Anderson. I, uh... own this house." She grimaced, her proclamation earning her the exact reaction she'd expected.

"That cannot be correct! This is *my* home! I–" Vasile stopped, raking his fingers through his hair. "Someone must have taken it over, assuming I abandoned it. Bastards."

It didn't help that the house *definitely* looked nothing like it had when Vasile lived there. The man who sold it to her bragged that everything was refinished, which she believed. The place still smelled vaguely like a construction zone.

"Just don't be mad at *me* about it, okay? You owe me one, considering I'm not mad at you for attacking me." She stared at him pointedly, and his already pale features flushed as if suddenly remembering what he'd done.

"Ah... I promise, I can explain–"

"You can explain while I show you around the house. C'mon." She guided him up the stairs, following behind him to spot him as he climbed the stairs on unsteady legs.

Luckily, the sun had fully dipped below the horizon by the time they made it upstairs. It wasn't entirely nighttime yet, but if Vasile was bothered by what little daylight lingered, he didn't mention it. "This... does not even *look* like my house," he breathed as Haley closed the door behind them. "But there are small things–my fireplace!" He dashed through the living room to the old stone fireplace and crouched, tracing his fingers over the brick. "I would not believe this was the same building if not for this fireplace. And it is just as lovely as I remember."

Haley's chest tightened. She couldn't imagine how terrified he must be. Even just moving from the south to the north felt like a massive culture shock. Just a few hours ago, she'd been offended that the barista at Dunkin hadn't said 'have a nice day' to her.

"Pretty bird!" Brenda squawked from her perch inside her cage, rustling her feathers indignantly. Much the opposite of her mother, Brenda was an attention whore. She was probably pissed that Haley and Vasile had spent more than thirty seconds in the room without speaking to her.

Vasile's head jerked in Brenda's direction. "Oh, my, you *are* a pretty bird," he said, fireplace forgotten as he crossed the floor to Brenda. "You look so much like my Myrtle."

Something like warmth blossomed in the middle of Haley's chest. "Did you have a bird, too?"

"I did. The loveliest little budgerigar. She was quite the talker." He offered the crook of his finger to Brenda and she happily hopped onto it, allowing Vasile to smooth his finger over the top of her head. "As are you, I assume."

"Are you a cop?" Brenda chirped, and Vasile raised an eyebrow.

"A cop?"

This fucking bird. "She's asking if you're a police officer," Haley said, trying and failing to hide her amusement.

Vasile placed a hand to his chest in what appeared to be abject horror. "I certainly am not."

"Cop!" But she rubbed her head against his fingertip anyway, and Haley was suddenly glad Brenda wasn't a watch dog.

Haley tried not to let herself wonder about what had happened to Myrtle in Vasile's absence as he continued to stroke her head. "So, you gonna explain the whole 'attacking me' thing now?" she asked.

Vasile attempted to stop petting Brenda, but she wasn't having it. She nipped at his finger as he pulled it away. "Yes, I... suppose I should." He didn't look at Haley as he spoke. "I assume you have put the pieces together that I am not an ordinary person, as ordinary people do not tend to sleep for two centuries without consequence."

"Definitely not."

"I am an immortal creature," he said, and Haley couldn't help but think he looked like the hero of a tragic Gothic horror film as he stared out the window, bird perched on his finger. "Though, I will say, I have never slept for so long... a week, perhaps, but over two hundred years?" Brenda bobbed her head, as if listening to him. "As for the attack... I fear there is no easy way for me to say it."

Haley found herself marginally less excited for the whole 'vampire' reveal than she had been before. "Well, there's not much you could say that's weirder than 'I took a nap for two hundred years,'" she pointed out.

Vasile let out a mirthful laugh. "Oh, I am certain you are wrong about that." Brenda flitted back to her perch and he dropped his hand. "Human food does not sustain me anymore. I require blood, and

I believe that is what finally roused me from my slumber. Your blood smells particularly... alluring."

Please, Haley, be so normal about this. Haley cleared her throat. "Or you're just *really* malnourished from two centuries of starvation."

"That certainly could be the case," Vasile said. "On that matter... I should probably hunt. Nightfall is approaching."

"Wait," Haley said before her brain could tell her not to. She didn't love the idea of him running out into a New York that he certainly didn't know, hunting down... what, squirrels? Or worse, *actual* people?

She worried her lower lip between her teeth. "You could bite me. If you wanted to. I mean, y'know, to hold you over until you can...." Her resolve fizzled out. *Stupid.* This was a stupid thing to suggest. They'd only just learned each other's names, and offering to let a vampire drink her blood was–

"Are you certain?" Vasile's eyes almost seemed to flash darker red now. "I feel I must warn you...

I have never gone this long without sustenance before. I trust that I will not lose control, but I cannot promise such."

Haley's mouth ran dry, which very much could be from that second half of weed gummy. But it could *definitely* also be because Vasile was staring at her with a hunger she didn't know she could draw from another human being. "It's okay. Brenda can supervise," she joked half-heartedly, and Brenda gave an affirmative caw.

"Promise me you will tell me to stop if you become light-headed," he said, taking a step closer to her.

"I will," she said. Vasile closed the distance between them, brushing the dark brown hair from her shoulder with a brush of his cold hand. She could have sworn she heard his breath catch as he leaned in.

And then, his teeth were on her neck.

Chapter Four

B eing bitten by a vampire wasn't anything like Haley expected, and it *certainly* wasn't anything like it was depicted in her smutty paranormal romance books.

Vasile's fangs piercing her skin stung and he immediately soothed the bite with his tongue before latching on. She bit back a whimper–of what, she didn't know–and clutched his upper arms for support. This time, he didn't reject her touch. He circled an arm around her waist, supporting her weight.

It took a surprisingly short amount of time for her to feel dizziness blurring the edges of her vision. But she didn't want him to stop. Why, she didn't know. But it took every ounce of her self control to bat at his shoulder. "Vasile," she breathed. When he didn't stop immediately, she tried again. "Vasile!"

He pulled away from her with a gasp, but didn't withdraw his arm from around her. "My apologies. I thought I might have better control of myself than that," he said, voice strained as he fought to catch his breath. He brushed a thumb over the bite mark and pulled back his blood-smeared thumb. Haley felt as if her heart might burst straight through her ribcage as he licked the red from the pad of his finger. This man was *actually* going to be the death of her. And she'd probably let him. "Are you alright?"

"Never better." She blinked back the spots in her vision, fighting to maintain her composure as Vasile pulled his arm away from her.

His eyes had returned to what Haley assumed was their normal shade; hazel, flecked with yellow.

Her own dark brown eyes felt particularly plain in comparison. "I hope you do not mind my saying this, but there is... an odd taste to your blood."

"Yeah, it's probably all the weed," Haley grimaced. "But, hey, maybe it'll help with your hangover."

"Weed? You mean to say you have consumed... plants?"

Haley fought back a chuckle. "Uh... cannabis?"

That seemed to click with Vasile. "You have consumed hashish?"

"Are you a cop?" Brenda chimed in, and Haley failed to withhold her laughter this time. The force of it made her stumble, and Vasile reached out to steady her.

"I have to admit, my headache has dulled," he said. "Perhaps you should lie down."

Laying down would be a *great* idea if she'd gone out to the store to buy a mattress like she was supposed to. But she'd spent most of her sober hours constructing Brenda's new enclosure, and then Rhea had distracted her. Right now, her only option for laying down was on the cold hardwood, which didn't sound terribly appealing. Her body was already running concerningly cold.

Vasile seemed to mirror her concern. "Do you... have no furniture?" he asked her.

"Guilty." She raised her hands in surrender. "I just moved in today." Vasile *had* to be regretting waking up right about now.

"Might you have a friend who can construct a bedstead for you?" he asked. "I might have had a recommendation for a seamstress two hundred years ago... where might you obtain a featherbed?"

Haley was a little too delirious for this. "There might still be a furniture store open...," she murmured, slipping her phone out of her pocket. She'd only just unlocked it when Vasile leaped away from her as if she'd shocked him.

"What *is* that?" he asked breathlessly. Something told Haley she was going to be hearing a *lot* of that from him.

"A phone." She turned the screen toward him and he immediately squinted his eyes against it. There probably wasn't anything this bright back in the 1800s. "Pretty much everyone has one nowadays. I can use it to call my friends, or just send them messages, and then there's the internet, which–" Her words died in her throat. Actually, she wasn't sure she had the mental energy to explain the entirety of the internet to him. "Long story short, these things can do everything."

"Incredible. I have missed so much," Vasile said, and the unmistakable sadness in his voice made Haley's throat hurt. "So we can retrieve a bed for you tonight?"

"Yeah. Should be able to fit it in the truck." She tapped on the GPS directions for the furniture store that was open the latest–a Discount Furniture only three miles away–and shoved her phone into her pocket. "I need to go change. Wait for me right here." Her eyes flicked to Brenda. "Don't eat Brenda, okay?"

Vasile harrumphed. "How rude of you to insinuate. I would eat *you* sooner than I would eat Brenda."

She *definitely* didn't have time to unpack how that made her feel. She dashed for her bedroom as quickly as her still swimming head would allow her and shut the door, rubbing at her temples.

There was a vampire in her house. And she'd let him *drink from her.* And she'd... liked it? Not only was Rhea never going to believe her, she was also *never* going to let Haley live this down.

She threw on a pair of jeans and her Emory University sweatshirt and stepped into the bathroom to freshen up. Today had felt like an entire week, and she *looked* like she'd lived an entire week. The bags under her eyes were darker than she'd ever seen them, and even the freckles dotting her cheeks seemed to have paled. Her dark brown hair hung about her face limply, as if it were just as tired as she was. She gave her cheeks a pinch in an attempt to breathe life back into them and not look quite so much like a walking corpse.

When Haley returned to the living room, Vasile was staring out the window. She came to stand next to him, her gaze following his. The sky was dark now, the moon and stars completely obscured by clouds. Car headlights whizzed by, the reflection of them gleaming in Vasile's eyes.

"You okay?" she asked him.

"Yes." He tucked his hands behind his back, stepping away from the window. "Shall we?"

"Okay. But just prepare yourself, because I'm about to take you out in my truck." She grabbed her purse from its spot on the floor next to the door and slung it over her shoulder. Vasile didn't seem terribly phased by that, if only because he hadn't the slightest idea of what a truck was. She opened the door for him, the warm summer breeze a welcome introduction to her chilled skin.

He barely made it a foot out the door before he froze in place. "Is this meant to be a carriage?" he asked, placing a testing hand on the hood of her truck. "It is an ugly thing, isn't it?"

Okay, maybe it was a *little* ugly, but only Haley was allowed to say that. She'd had the damned thing since she was twenty, and the fact that it had still survived the drive up to New York was a miracle. "Hey, be nice to her," she said, rubbing a soothing hand over one of the mirrors. "She's been through a lot."

"I can see that." He chipped off a flake of rusted purple paint with a fingernail, and she shot him a sideways glance. "How does it move?"

"You'll see." She rounded the truck to the passenger side and opened the door, bowing before it. "After you, m'sir."

The corner of Vasile's lips quirked into a smile. "I do not think that is correct, but thank you," he said, but climbed in, Haley resting a hand on the small of his back to support him. She only just caught his little jump as the heavy door closed beside him.

When she got in, he was admiring every knob on the dashboard. "What do all of these controls do?" he asked. He turned the volume knob on the radio experimentally, a quizzical look crossing his features when nothing happened. Haley grinned.

"You'll see." She turned the key in the ignition and the truck roared to life, earning a squeal of surprise from Vasile. *Cute.*

He clutched the arm rests with a white-knuckled grip, raising himself off the seat a few inches.

"Is it normal for your carriages to shake so aggressively?" he asked, his voice raising an octave.

Maybe hers was a *little* more aggressive than cars tended to be. It wasn't her fault her truck was old as dirt. "You'll get used to it, I promise," she said. "Sit down. Lemme put your seatbelt on you so you don't die."

"The likelihood of your carriage being the cause of my death is slim," Vasile said primly, but did as he was told. His grip on the arm rests didn't falter.

"I promise you, it's not." She leaned over him for his seatbelt and, for a second, their eyes met. He smiled at her properly this time—a smile that was probably more nerves than anything, but a smile nonetheless. "This'll keep you safe."

"I am choosing to trust in your carriage driving skills," Vasile said, allowing her another one of his small smiles.

Haley could feel the blush creeping onto her cheeks. "Yeah, well, trusting me with anything isn't the brightest idea." She buckled his seatbelt and shoved herself back into her own seat as quickly as she could, trying not to let herself think too much about how gorgeous Vasile was up close.

Once they were properly on the road, Vasile seemed to relax more, though his shoulders were still visibly tense. "You wanna see what all these buttons do?" she asked in an attempt to distract him.

"Oh, yes!" Vasile said. Haley turned the radio on and once again startled him. If this poor guy's heart was still beating, he probably would have had a heart attack by now. The radio was already tuned to Haley's usual station, playing the current chart toppers. She turned the volume dial down, and Vasile's eyes widened to an almost comical degree. "What advanced technology. Is there anything this carriage *cannot* do?"

"Well, a back up camera would be nice," Haley muttered. "And Bluetooth." Vasile turned a questioning eye to her. The technology education was going to have to wait for Haley's brain to return to normal. "So, what's the last thing you remember? Before the whole two hundred year long nap?"

Vasile jabbed one of the preset buttons on the radio, switching it to the news station Haley listened to on the rare occasion that she felt mentally stable enough to learn about what was going on in the world. Luckily, Vasile's voice drowned out the radio. "I was not lying about the laudanum. But it was more like... I was feeding on a person who had taken a *lot* of it."

"Party boy, huh?" Haley teased.

He experimented with the tuning dial, static filling the air between them. "Oh, not at all. I did not go out often. This was... a momentary lapse in judgment." The tone of his voice made her *really* not want to pry.

"Happens to the best of us." She chewed the inside of her cheek. "Sorry I bought your house."

Vasile laughed, a sound that Haley was really starting to appreciate. "It is not your fault. You did not know. And in any case, I am grateful that you did. I might have been sleeping a lot longer had you not been the one to purchase my home."

The thought of Vasile being trapped in the basement of his own home, his existence lost to time made her heart drop into her stomach. "Glad I could be of service," she said.

Vasile changed the radio again, and this time, piano music filtered through the speakers. He sat back, drumming his fingertips on his thighs as if he were playing the piano. He *looked* like someone who should play the piano.

She took a wrong turn just before they reached the furniture store to allow him just another minute of peace.

Chapter Five

All things considered, the trip to the furniture store could have gone a lot worse.

And honestly, watching Vasile's growing fascination over the different types of mattresses was… cute. It was a good thing Haley was barely high anymore, or else she absolutely wouldn't have been able to contain her laughter when Vasile asked the salesman if he had woven the mattress fabric himself.

Haley was more than happy to settle with the cheapest mattress and frame set she could find, but Vasile seemed to take that personally. "This is a bed for *children*, Haley," he'd admonished her when she decided on a twin mattress and a frame just a step above laying the mattress on the floor. "You are the head of your household. You deserve the utmost comfort."

She didn't have the strength to remind him that it was *her* credit card they were swiping, not his, so she ended up with a modest queen bed and a frame that gave her decent storage space under the bed. Not that she really needed it. Brenda would probably just hide out under there after stealing snacks from the pantry.

Vasile hardly even allowed her to help bring the furniture out to the truck. She'd only helped with the mattress to save it from dragging on the concrete through the parking lot. And when they returned to Haley's house, she didn't try quite as hard not to stare at Vasile openly as he lugged the box containing the frame into the house with seemingly no issue.

"How strange, putting your wood inside more wood to transport it to your home," Vasile said as he unpacked the frame from its box. "This seems wasteful."

Haley snorted. "Welcome to the 2000s. Everything's wasteful." She sat next to Vasile, cross-legged, and pored over the instructions.

Vasile made a humming sound under his breath. "How are these meant to be of any assistance to us?" he asked, turning the packet of screws over in his hands. "These are meant for building?"

"Oh! We need a drill!" Something told Haley this was yet another thing Vasile was going to *hate*. "Hold on." She retrieved her power drill from one of the boxes. Rhea had personally ensured Haley had one, tucking it into her box the day before she left.

Which would be more helpful if Haley had any idea how to use it. She held it up, and Vasile stared at it as if it might leap out and bite him. "This thing!" She pressed the trigger and the drill buzzed, eliciting a yelp of surprise from Vasile.

"Why must everything be so loud?" he grunted, ripping open the bag of screws. While Haley tried to make sense of the instructions, Vasile laid out the various planks of wood. "Ah, I see. The small pieces of metal connect the slats of wood... might I borrow your tool?"

Haley raised her brows. "You sure? You looked like you were gonna pee your pants a second ago."

Vasile huffed, reaching for the drill. "I can assure you I was at no risk of wetting my trousers." He took it from her, his icy fingers brushing hers. Despite the cold, she still felt the burn of his touch for a few seconds after. He grimaced at the whirr of the drill as he attached the two slats of wood, wringing his hands once he set the drill on the floor. "Effective, but absolutely horrible."

Haley giggled, sliding closer to him. "How about you let me take care of that part?"

"I've got it." His words weren't *entirely* believable, but she let him. "Might you have somewhere I can hang my coat?" he asked after drilling in the second set of screws, which he seemed marginally less terrified of. "It is impeding my movement."

Coathangers might have been a good thing to invest in, but Haley was particularly guilty of tossing her clothes wherever they landed and hoping she remembered where they were the next day. "Sure," she said, shoving herself to her feet. Vasile slipped his coat off and passed it to her, leaving him in a pressed white button-up with frilled cuffs. It was heavy in her hands, and she smoothed her thumbs over the soft velvet. This thing had to cost a fortune.

There went her idea of draping it across the floor as tidily as she could. She pursed her lips and settled with opening the door just enough to hang the jacket from the top of it. When she turned back around, Vasile looked particularly unimpressed, but spared her the lecture.

"So, you were a doctor back in Transylvania?" Haley asked, using the hair tie on her wrist to pull her hair back and out of her face. She took the drill back from him, to spare his delicate hands and ears.

"Yes, I was." He twisted a screw in with his fingers, which Haley learned quickly was her cue to go in with the drill. "I owned a practice with a few other doctors. I traveled to America to further my education."

"*Further* your education? God, I couldn't make it through a *year* of college, never mind the probably *ten* you did."

Vasile's eyes widened a fraction. "You attended university? Women are allowed to?"

Suddenly, being alive in the year 2026 didn't feel quite so terrible. "Yep. The women from your time would probably be ashamed of me, giving it up like I did," she laughed.

"University is not for everyone," Vasile said simply, and it was Haley's turn to be surprised. She found herself staring at him as he unwrapped another slat of wood from its plastic. "I am lucky, I suppose, in the sense that my field of study has been a fixation of mine since I was a child. I learned how to read by reading my father's medical texts. I doubt I will ever tire of learning about the field of medicine." He tossed the plastic away from him, flexing his fingers as if to rid them of the sensation. "Though, I suppose I have a lot to learn now. I cannot imagine how much medicine has developed in my absence."

Haley took the liberty of unwrapping the rest of the wood while Vasile sat back, unclasping his cuffs and rolling his sleeves up. His long, pale arms were practically hairless and just as elegant as the rest of him. "Just you wait. Hospitals are probably *way* louder now than they were back then," she said, and Vasile's nose wrinkled. "What kind of medicine did you do?"

"As much of it as I could. I have a particular interest in endocrinology, but there is no facet of medicine that I do not wish to learn about." Vasile held a hand out. "May I try again with the drill?"

She passed him the drill and couldn't help but smile at his awkward grip. "Here. Hold it like this." She wrapped her hands around his, adjusting his grip around the handle. "Then you'll have more control over it.

"Oh." The sound was breathless, and when he glanced up at her, she could have sworn her heart forgot how to beat. Now that his eyes weren't red with hunger anymore, they were more green than anything, with halos of warm brown surrounding his pupils. As if reading her mind, he said quietly,

"Your eyes are quite pretty. Has anyone ever told you they are the color of autumn leaves?"

Haley felt the blush creep onto her cheeks. "Nope. Can't say I've been told that before."

"Hm. Shame." He looked away, returning his attention to the wood in his lap. It took Haley a beat longer to reorient herself, the drill buzzing around them. "Autumn in Transylvania is beautiful. New York has its charm, but... it is no Transylvania."

Haley's heart lurched. "Do you miss it?"

"I do." Vasile didn't flinch as he drilled in the frame's final screw. "Once I have oriented myself, I must figure out how to get back. Perhaps... you could assist me with booking passage on a ship?"

Haley's smile was half-hearted, and she hoped Vasile couldn't tell. Getting attached to him was stupid. Selfish, even. She had no right to wish even for a second that he might consider staying here. "Yeah, of course. Except it might not be a ship." He tilted his head at her quizzically. "Let's get this mattress down."

They laid the mattress across the frame with a resounding *thump,* and Haley sat on the edge of it, bouncing a little. "Thanks for helping me put this together."

"It was my pleasure. Thank you for teaching me how to use a drill." Vasile sat next to her, folding his hands tidily in his lap. "And for... everything else. I hope that I have not been an inconvenience on your evening."

"You haven't, I promise," Haley said easily. "It's been weird, but fun."

"You are alarmingly calm about things." Vasile offered her a small smile. "I am envious of that. I do not know that I have ever been calm a day in my life."

"No offense, but I can tell," she said, and he laughed, a soft, sweet laugh that he covered with his fingertips. God, she was in trouble. She stood up and retrieved Vasile's jacket from the door. "Alright, you got to eat, but I haven't eaten in a few hours. So you're coming with me to get some food."

"Of course. It is the least I could do." Vasile slipped his jacket back on, and Haley immediately missed the sight of his forearms. "Will anything be open at this time of night?"

"Trust me, *everything* will be open." She peered down at her phone for the first time in a few hours. It was only one in the morning, which was still pretty early for her.

A wall of notifications blocked the lower half of her phone screen, each one from Rhea. The messages gradually increased in desperation.

RHEA: what happened with the dead guy?

RHEA: are YOU dead?

RHEA: that was supposed to be a joke, you better not be fucking dead

RHEA: HALEY CHRISTINE ANDERSON IF YOU DONT TEXT ME BACK IN TWO MINUTES

The twenty-seven missed calls mirrored her threat. Had she really been so wrapped up in hanging out with a *boy* that she'd managed to somehow miss twenty-seven missed calls' worth of vibrations in her pocket?

HALEY: im still alive dont worry

HALEY: also, i was right :3c

She only just saw Rhea's message come through before she shoved her phone back into her pocket.

RHEA: oh my god you are actually gonna be the death of me. call me when you can, PLEASE

She could call Rhea later. Right now, she was in desperate need of sustenance. "Alright. Let's go."

Chapter Six

Vasile didn't seem to hate being in the truck as much the second time around. He only spent about half of the entire drive clutching the arm rests for dear life, which felt like a win in Haley's book. By the time he'd come to a fully relaxed position in his seat, Haley was turning into the parking lot of the Mexican restaurant she'd become entirely too dependent on in the less-than twenty-four hours that she'd lived here.

She rounded the side of the building to the drive-thru speaker. "Do you want anything?" she asked him. "I mean... *can* you eat regular food?"

Vasile blinked, peering past her at the speaker. "I *can,* but I do not require it. Perhaps I will join you, though I fear the currency I hold will not work anymore."

"It's okay. It's my treat." Something told Haley Vasile wouldn't have the slightest idea what to order at a Mexican restaurant, so she ordered a variation of tacos, a horchata, and a pineapple agua fresca. Hopefully, he'd like *something.*

The moment the static from the other end of the speaker cut out, Vasile leaned over. "How is that possible?" he stage-whispered. "That person surely does not fit inside this box."

Haley grinned. "Once we get our food, we'll eat and I'll give you a whoooole lesson about today's technology." She pulled up to the window, earning a knowing stare from the worker that she had only seen a couple hours ago. Luckily, she was polite enough not to point it out. Haley tasked Vasile with holding the food, and he tugged at her sleeve just as she was saying her thanks.

"They must have made a mistake," Vasile said. "This cannot be our food. That was too quick."

"Welcome to the new world, Vasile. We're all about instant gratification." She circled the parking lot and backed the truck into one of the parking spots tucked in the darkest corner of the lot, away from the beam of the street lights. "Come on. We're gonna sit back here." She helped Vasile out of the truck before grabbing their drinks and plopping them in the truck's bed.

"Back where?" he asked.

"Here." Haley released the tailgate and hopped into the truck. She took the greasy bag of food from him and held her hands out. "Hop up. I'll help you."

Vasile looked a bit like she'd just asked him to chop all of his hair off, but he obliged, placing his small, cold hands in hers and jumping into the truck. He stumbled in Haley's grip and she caught him, arms around his waist. His chest came to rest against hers for such a brief second that Haley lost the opportunity to appreciate his closeness. "Thank you," he mumbled before pulling out of her grip. "Might you have something I can sit on?

This coat was... well, rather expensive, you see, and–"

"Say less, my prince," Haley said, tugging off her sweatshirt and laying it down in the bed of the truck. She couldn't blame him. This bed *was* pretty dirty and, at this time of year, coated in leaves and twigs from the shedding trees.

Vasile's eyes flicked to her now-bare arms. She was only wearing a black tank top now, and the autumn air bit at her skin. "Will you not be cold?" he asked.

"I'll be okay." She sat cross-legged next to the sweatshirt and took the paper bag into her lap. "I got a bunch of stuff because I didn't know what you'd like. You've probably never had Mexican food before, right?"

"I have not, but it smells delightful," Vasile said, accepting one of the giant styrofoam cups Haley passed him.

"Try that. It's called agua fresca. That one's, like, rice and cinnamon?" She claimed the lengua taco and the chorizo before passing a carnitas taco to him.

He balanced the foil-wrapped taco on his knee, focusing his energy instead on the cup in his hands. He gave the straw an experimental tug, and Haley fought to suppress her laughter. *Oh my God. He's never used a straw before.*

"Just suck on it. You're a vampire, you're good at that," she teased, taking a sip of the pineapple agua fresca.

"This is *very* different," Vasile said indignantly, but followed Haley's lead. The crease between his brows immediately dissolved away with a sip of horchata. "Oh, that is delicious."

"I know." It was her favorite but, just this once, she'd leave it for him. This was probably the only time they'd ever be able to share food like this. She cleared her throat as if to clear the thought from her mind as well. She stuck her cup between her legs and unwrapped her chorizo taco, giving it a generous squeeze of lime and dousing it in hot sauce.

Vasile started to unwrap his taco and glanced sideways at her. "You are *definitely* cold," he said.

"You can sit closer to me, if you would like. I am not warm myself, but my coat certainly is."

Haley wasn't really in a position to say no. Eating tacos was kind of hard to do with trembling fingers that she was slowly losing feeling in. "Thanks," she said and moved closer to him. She tucked herself against the fabric of his coat, which was somehow even warmer than she'd anticipated.

Vasile took a bite and let out a satisfied sigh. "It has been so long since I have consumed human food. I forgot how delicious it could be." He wrapped the taco up after his first bite and shrugged out of his coat. "Here. You need this more than I do." He draped it around her shoulders and she gathered the fabric at the bottom in an attempt to keep it safe from her filthy truck.

All of the chill in her body immediately disappeared. It didn't have the lingering warmth that a jacket borrowed from someone else might normally have, but it *did* smell like Vasile, a fact that she tried not to let herself enjoy too much. His smell was clean more than anything, with an underlying almost medicinal herbaceousness that she found herself enjoying.

"What if your expensive coat gets dirty?" she asked, feeling wholly unworthy of allowing it to rest around her shoulders.

"I trust you to keep it safe." He traced a thumb across the shiny aluminum. "You have not told me much about yourself. I feel that I must have bored you with so much talk of what my life was like before this."

"Trust me, you're a lot more interesting than I am," Haley said, wadding up her foil and tossing it into the bag. "I'm no smart Transylvanian doctor."

Vasile clicked his tongue. "What good is a doctor who is two centuries behind modern medicine?" He took another sip of horchata, the ridiculously huge cup dwarfing his already small hands. "If you are no, as you say, smart Transylvanian doctor... what *are* you?"

Haley shrugged. "A starving artist?"

Vasile chuckled, the sound rumbling in his chest. "Ah, so some things have not changed in the centuries. I thought we might have developed more respect for the arts by now."

"Tragically, no." Haley drizzled hot sauce on her lengua taco and licked a trail of hot sauce off her thumb. Maybe she was imagining things, but she could have sworn Vasile watched the swipe of her tongue. "I sell TV and internet over the phone so I can afford to buy painting supplies." Her head came to rest against Vasile's shoulder, and he didn't brush her off. "But it's sucking the life out of me. I get so tired from talking to people all day that I just... lay around and watch TV or play on my phone all night instead of *making* anything."

Vasile went quiet, save for a quiet slurp from his drink. "I am sorry. I cannot imagine how frustrating that must be. Have you any pictures of your art on that little box of yours?"

Haley hadn't shown anyone her art in years. Even Rhea had never seen any of it. She'd squirreled away the very few paintings she'd produced over the time she and Rhea lived together, and she'd left them all behind. Except for one.

But if Vasile was going to disappear from her life after tonight, she could show him. In a hundred years, he wouldn't remember her or her art. "I do," she said, tugging her phone out of her back pocket and flicking through her photo album. She rifled through the pictures until she found a photo of the last piece she'd created and *didn't* hate. A portrait of Rhea.

"I did this portrait of my best friend... I think three years ago now," Haley said, turning the screen towards Vasile. He squinted against it initially before relaxing, leaning into her to peer down at her phone.

It was an oil painting, one of a bright-faced, blue-haired Rhea surrounded by peonies, her favorite flower. Looking at it now, she didn't hate it quite as much as she had back then. "It was supposed to be a birthday gift for her, but I just wasn't happy with it. I don't think I was happy with anything I did back then."

"What do you mean?" Vasile gasped, almost as if he was *actually* offended. "Haley, this is beautiful. Your friend has not seen it?"

Haley shook her head. "Nope. It's gonna stay in my bedroom forever."

"What a shame. The world is much less beautiful without it," Vasile said solemnly and popped the last of his taco into his mouth. Haley turned to look at him, but he was staring straight ahead, the reflection of the night sky dancing in his eyes.

"Thanks," Haley said quietly. She moved closer to him still, the tip of her sneaker brushing against the polished leather of his boot. He draped an arm around her and she took it as the opportunity to return the favor, her arm around his middle.

"I have never been an artistic person. I fear I do not have a creative bone in my body," he said, and Haley laughed. "I am always in awe of artists. Of how you can look at another being and see something other than cells and skin and hair. I can only imagine the great privilege it might be to be loved by an artist." He rested his cheek against the top of her head. "Your friend is lucky to have you."

Haley stared down at his joined hands, the deep purple veins branching under the pale skin, and wondered how anyone could see anything but art in him.

Chapter Seven

Haley *really* needed to call Rhea.

Rhea had always been the most grounded of the two, maybe sometimes to a detrimental extent. And while Haley was more of what Rhea would call an airhead, she didn't generally get herself into situations that required more grounding than she could give herself.

Except for now. Thinking that she could possibly be falling in love with a centuries-old vampire that she'd met all of five hours ago required grounding that Haley couldn't provide.

"I need to make a phone call real quick," Haley said to Vasile once they were back in the living room. Brenda chirped a greeting at them, and Vasile was all too happy to approach her cage, offering a finger to her. "I'll be right back."

Her cell phone was at her ear the second she shut her bedroom door behind her. Rhea answered on the first ring. "Oh my God, you're alive," Rhea said in what sounded like one breath. "What the fuck is going on, Haley? I've been freaking out *all night.*"

Haley sucked in a breath. Where could she start that wasn't 'well, I'm in love with a vampire, I think?' "Remember when I said I was right? In the text message?"

"Yeah. Super vague. Thanks for that."

"What I meant was that I was right about the whole... vampire thing. He's a vampire."

The line went so quiet, Haley wondered if Rhea had hung up on her. "Shut the fuck up. You're lying to me."

Haley crossed her heart despite the fact that Rhea couldn't see it. "I swear on my life, I wouldn't lie about a vampire."

She could practically feel Rhea's stare on her. "Okay, okay, you met a *vampire*? One that was living in your *house*?"

Haley grimaced. "Well, technically, it's *his* house. He owned it, like, in the 1800s. He's just been asleep in the basement this entire time."

"Shit. Maybe we should've been worried about *you* having squatter's rights." Rhea huffed, and Haley could barely make out the squeak of a mattress. "Okay, well... what're you gonna do about this whole thing?"

Haley slid to the floor, her back against the door. "I don't know." She didn't know that she *wanted* to do anything about it. She couldn't kick Vasile out of his house. It was his *way* before it was hers. And leaving meant going back to Atlanta, which wasn't the worst possible outcome, but she didn't like how the thought of leaving him felt.

"Okay, different question. What does *he* want?" Rhea asked, her voice softer now.

A lump formed at the back of Haley's throat. "I think he wants to go home," she said, her tacos starting to revolt in her stomach. "To Transylvania. Romania. Whatever. He was a doctor, and he came over here to study way back in the day."

"Oh!" The relief in Rhea's voice did little to soothe Haley. "Okay, problem solved! He goes back home, you stay in the house, it's all good!"

"Yeah," Haley croaked, tears prickling at her sinuses. She couldn't hold him back, and she knew that. He was too intelligent of a man to give up on his dreams for a woman he'd known for a night, and she wouldn't dream of asking him to do so.

Rhea sighed, and Haley knew exactly what was coming. "You're not happy about that arrangement, are you?" she asked softly. Haley only sniffed in response. "God, only *I* would get stuck with a best friend who could fall in love with a vampire that she found sleeping in her house."

Haley laughed despite herself, dabbing at her eyelashes with the pads of her fingers. "If you saw him, you'd get it. He's really hot."

"Whatever." Rhea blew out a breath that crackled through the phone. "Just talk to him. Maybe he's fine with staying in America. You never know."

Haley didn't *want* to talk to him. She wasn't prepared for his answer. Maybe she could pretend for the rest of the night that this wasn't happening, that she wasn't *actually* at risk of losing him. That she didn't care about losing him. "Yeah. Yeah, maybe he *will* stay here. I mean, he doesn't know how the world works yet. He's got a lot of learning to do before he goes anywhere."

"And who better to teach him than the sexy woman he already lives with?"

Haley laughed. "I guess so. I mean, he *is* ridiculously smart. He could probably figure it all out without me."

"You'd be surprised. Smartphones aren't all that intuitive nowadays," Rhea said. "God, a *vampire...* what a fucking day."

"You're telling me." Haley tugged at a stray thread at the hem of her tank top. "Is this crazy? To like this guy this much?"

"A little. But it's you. I wouldn't expect anything less." Rhea blew a kiss into the phone. "I need to get some sleep. But I love you, okay? No matter what happens."

"I love you, too." The line went dead and Haley buried her face into her knees. Rhea was right. This *was* crazy. But accidentally waking up a vampire who had been asleep for two hundred years was *also* pretty crazy, so maybe this situation called for a little crazy.

She wiped the last of her tears from her cheeks before returning to the living room. "Sorry. Rhea was just calling to check on me, and I–"

Vasile was crouched by the fireplace with Brenda perched on his shoulder, poking at the embers with a long iron rod that Haley had never seen before. His long curls were free from the confines of their ties, the ribbon now tied around his slender wrist. The whole living room felt a few degrees warmer now, and Haley couldn't tell if it was because of the fire or if her cheeks were just that hot.

"Is everything alright?" he asked, pushing himself to his feet. "I hope you do not mind that I put a fire on."

Everything *wasn't* alright. The domesticity of all of this made her want to cry again. "No, no, the fire's good," Haley said, her voice betraying her.

"I'm okay. I just needed to check in with Rhea. I was on the phone with her when I found you, so... she was freaking out a little."

"Ah. That is only fair." His expression shifted as she approached him. "Have you been crying?"

The confirmation only managed to break the flimsy dam holding her tears back. They streamed down her cheeks freely now, and she laughed past them. "I thought I was doing such a good job at hiding them."

"Come sit by the fire with me." He guided her by the elbow back toward the fireplace and sat, cross-legged, pulling Haley down beside him. She sat so close to him their thighs brushed. "What is the matter?"

How could she tell him she was scared of him leaving when she couldn't even pinpoint why? She'd *dated* people for longer than this and been less affected by losing them.

But there was something about Vasile. Something about him drew her to him, made every cell in her stupid body want to be as close to him as possible. It was like her soul knew something about him that she didn't, like there was something cosmic that put them here, together, tonight.

Or maybe all of that cosmic stuff was bullshit and she was just a pathetic girl falling head over heels for the first man that was even a little nice to her. It had been the same with Camille, with all of the shitty guys she'd dated in her early twenties. A few nice words, a few lingering touches, and she was a goner.

"It's nothing," she tried. "It's just... y'know, all the weed."

"I may not have partaken myself, but I am quite certain this is not a hashish side effect." In a surprisingly tender motion, he took one of her warm hands between his. "I apologize. It is late now, and all of this must be terribly frustrating for you–"

"God, the only frustrating part of this is how *nice* you are." She stared down at his hands enveloping hers. "I'm really enjoying tonight with you. Like, a lot. You're... funny and interesting and charming and even my *bird* likes you and she doesn't like anyone!" Brenda gave her feathers a little shake like she resented the statement but, like a smart bird, didn't argue.

"It is not Brenda's fault she is particular about the company she keeps," Vasile said. He smoothed a thumb along the side of Haley's hand. "I... am enjoying my night with you as well. Greatly. You have taught me so much, and, if I might say so, you are the loveliest creature I have ever laid eyes on. I am finding myself..." He drew in a breath. "...Struggling at the thought of what might come after tonight."

The very thing Haley *really* didn't want to think about. "Me too." Her voice cracked, a single droplet landing on the top of Vasile's hand. "I don't wanna hold you back."

He withdrew the hand on top of hers and instead used it to brush her hair behind her ear. "I fear there is nothing in this world that might hold me back," he said quietly. "No matter how terribly my heart wishes it could."

"Wow. You're a really good person. You should be, like, a doctor or something," Haley laughed, but an inevitable sob strangled the sound. This time, Vasile was the one to wipe her tears away.

"We still have tonight," he said, and Haley lifted her head. "If you might have me for tonight."

Haley nodded. "I would like that," she whispered, and Vasile took her face gently between his hands, like he might break her. She sniffled, wrapping a hand around his wrist and giving it a squeeze, as if to remind herself that he was still there.

He leaned in and pressed his lips to hers, and Haley sunk into him.

Chapter Eight

Vasile didn't release Haley's face once their lips parted, and Haley wasn't sure she was ready to be any further away from him than this. She climbed into his lap and kissed him again, her arms draped over his shoulders. His fangs grazed her lower lip and Haley gasped, the metallic tang of iron settling onto her tongue.

"My apologies, Haley, I did not mean to harm you," Vasile whispered, soothing the bite with a swipe of his thumb.

"It didn't hurt." Haley pressed a kiss to the pad of his finger. "You can do it again, if you want."

But he didn't. He kissed her again, his fangs safely contained in his mouth, but Haley wanted to feel them on her again. She moved her hands to rest on his chest and he pulled back as if he'd been burned.

"Are you okay?" Haley asked, yanking her hands back just as quickly. "I didn't mean to–" She didn't really know what she meant to do. Maybe burrow her hands under every infuriating layer of clothing on him, dip them under his skin and imprint herself on the cells inside his body so he was biologically unable to forget her.

"I have to tell you something." This time, Vasile looked as if he might cry.

"Okay." Haley sat back, and Vasile wouldn't meet her eyes no matter how hard she tried to make him. He stared into his lap, one of his fists at his side clenching and unclenching.

"I have misled you. I... could not have possibly imagined that we would be at this point, or else I would have been honest with you from the start," he said. Haley couldn't imagine what secret he could possibly be hiding that could be worse than being a *vampire*. "I have lived as a man for most of my life. I would have likely done it as a child, had I been allowed. I thought for so long that I was doing this for the opportunity to attend university, but... that was simply not the case."

Oh. Haley's throat grew tight, and she immediately took both of his hands in hers. "You didn't mislead me, Vasile." She couldn't imagine what it might have been like two hundred years ago–it was hard enough for trans people *today,* never mind back then. "But thank you for telling me."

Vasile's head whipped up, his eyes wide as they met Haley's. "You are not concerned?"

"No." She brushed a curl out of his eyes. "You're a man, and that's all I need to know." She chewed her lower lip, resting both of her hands on his shoulders and skimming them under his coat, pushing it to the floor.

He didn't try to stop it from falling. "Haley...," he whispered. She didn't think she'd ever grow tired of how her name sounded on his tongue. "Thank you." He reached up to unclasp the buttons at his throat, and Haley helped with the rest.

The silky fabric fell to the floor with his coat, and the only thing covering Vasile now were bandages wrapped around his chest. She trailed the tips of her fingers over them and Vasile flinched.

"I would like to leave them on, if you don't mind," he said quietly, and Haley withdrew her hand, instead trailing her fingers down his stomach. Her hands found the button of his trousers and his breath caught in his throat. "Allow me to take you to bed. It is indecent to have you on the floor like this."

Well, if he said it like *that*, he could have her *anywhere*. "It's okay. I like indecent," she grinned, but Vasile rolled his eyes, allowing her to crawl off him before standing. She collected his jacket and allowed him to lead her by the hand back to her bedroom. Before stepping in, she hung his jacket over the door again.

"We should make your bed," Vasile said, appraising the bed before them. "I cannot imagine this would be comfortable without a cloth sheet. This fabric is truly horrible."

God, she should have just told him to fuck her on the floor. She opened her mouth to protest but he was already rummaging through the bag from the furniture store for the fitted sheet. He pulled it out, brows furrowing in confusion for a split second before attempting to put it on himself.

At least she couldn't say he wasn't a gentleman. She tucked in the two of the corners of the sheet that he hadn't, if only to draw his focus from the bed long enough to bring it back to her. "There," she said, perching on the edge of the bed. "This is good."

Vasile took the opportunity to nudge her knees apart with his, then rested his knee on the mattress between her legs. "I would disagree with that. I would rather have made the entire bed," he said, cradling one side of her face in one hand, "but if you are comfortable, then I will be, too."

Haley bit back the urge to whimper at the introduction of his leg between hers. "I'm more than comfortable," she managed, and allowed herself the smallest rock of her hips against him. He licked his lips at the sight of her, and she was pretty sure she was going to combust if he didn't touch her soon.

His hands found her hips, thumbs resting against her bare skin just under the hem of her shirt. "May I?" he asked, and Haley nodded, allowing him to slip her sweater off, leaving her in just a black tank top. He laid her sweatshirt across the bed next to them, as if she hadn't grabbed it out of a box in a wrinkled wad only a few hours ago. She suddenly wished she'd bothered to wear a nicer bra–or that she *had* a nicer bra to wear. Or one that fit her. Her cleavage spilled out of the top of this one, which looked nice while she was wearing the tank top but significantly *less* nice once she was out of it.

Vasile didn't seem to mirror that sentiment. "You are... breathtaking," he whispered, ducking his head to pepper kisses along her chest, her collarbone, the column of her throat. She swallowed against the feeling of his cold lips on her neck, and Vasile sucked in a sharp breath.

"You can bite me again, if you want," Haley managed. Truthfully, she just wanted to feel him all over her. His hands, his mouth, his fangs, his thigh–whatever he wanted.

"Perhaps." He fumbled with the clasps of her bra for a moment before Haley reached back and unclasped them herself. She could give him a little grace. Bras probably didn't exist back then. "I do not want to become too dependent on the taste of you."

Haley tossed her bra to the floor, her mouth running dry. How was she going to give this up? Give *him* up? She caught his head in her hands and pulled his face up to hers, swallowing his words with a kiss. He let out a small moan of surprise into her mouth, and she immediately knew she wanted to hear much, much more of that sound.

Vasile skimmed his hands down her torso and encouraged her back against the bed, crawling over her. His thigh pressed against her exactly where she needed him, and this time, she couldn't do much to stop the moan that escaped her.

A small smile tugged at the corners of his lips. "May I remove these?" he murmured, his voice huskier now. Haley nodded numbly, and he deftly unbuttoned her jeans and slid them down. She kicked them off and Vasile moved to, presumably, pick them up, but Haley wrapped an arm around his bicep.

"They're fine," she said breathlessly. "Stay here."

Vasile faltered but did as he was told, returning his attention to the bare skin of her stomach. He trailed kisses down the length of her, nipping the sensitive skin and soothing each bite with his tongue. She wished he'd bite harder, leave a few marks.

But he was agonizingly tender with her. He moved down her until he was nearly off the bed, pressing kisses to the insides of her thighs. She shifted up the bed to give him more room, suddenly finding herself grateful that he'd strong-armed her into a bigger mattress.

Vasile's fingertips dipped beneath the waistband of her underwear and pulled them down, leaving her fully bare before him. He took his time, revering every inch of her, encouraging her to hook her legs over his shoulders as his mouth finally found her begging, throbbing core.

His cold tongue on her was a shock to her heat, but God, did it feel good. "Shit, Vasile," she gasped, tangling her fingers in his dark curls. He gasped against her, and she gave his hair another experimental tug. His grip on her thighs tightened, as did her grip in his hair.

Vasile's tongue circled her expertly, the wet muscle soon joined by one of his fingers. He slid into her slowly, teasingly, while his mouth wrested loud, shameless cries of pleasure from her. She was never gonna be able to have sex with another man ever again. Vasile was *too* good.

"Very good, *dragă mea,*" he murmured against her as she pushed her hips into his hand. God, she was going to come *way* too fast, but he was infuriatingly good with his mouth. Another finger joined the first one inside her, both fingers curling and hitting a spot that made her arch her back off the bed.

"Vasile!" she cried out again, certain that if she kept tugging his hair so hard she would rip all of those pretty curls out. But she didn't stop. She was seeing stars, her toes curling with the effort of keeping her orgasm at bay for as long as she could.

Vasile's movements inside her picked up in voracity, his tongue on her never stilling. A fang caught the sensitive skin of her labia, the initial sting tangling with the all-consuming pleasure ravaging her.

She came against his tongue, her thighs clamping around his head as he lapped up her release like his life depended on it. Her entire body shuddered as he pulled his fingers out of her, and he moved up to position himself over her again. He leaned down, capturing her lips in a sloppy, sticky kiss, the taste of iron mingling with the taste of... herself.

This was by far the best orgasm she'd ever had, but she wasn't satiated. She wanted more of him. She wanted to hear *him* crying out, to see him lose himself in pleasure. "What can I do to you?" she whispered between hot, open-mouthed kisses.

"You need not worry about me." He kissed the underside of her jaw, her skin erupting in goosebumps at the sensation. "I do not enjoy much about the… pleasure receiving side of this. Much of it makes me quite uncomfortable."

"I have a dildo, if you want it," Haley said, and Vasile pulled his head back, eyebrows raised with shock.

"You do?" Vasile seemed to mull this over, and Haley took the opportunity to return the favor of lavishing him with kisses. She kissed every part of him she could reach, earning her a little whimper as her lips brushed his collarbone. "Might I see it?"

It took all of Haley's self-control to remove herself from him. She padded across the room to the singular box that contained all of her belongings. She only had two toys, and one of them got a *lot* more use than the other. But this one, she hoped, was perfect for the situation.

One end of it was shorter and thicker, the opposite end extending out into a normal dick shape. "This end goes inside you," she said, passing it to him with the shorter end facing him. "And then you can do whatever you want with the other end."

"Oh my." Vasile captured his lower lip between his teeth, and Haley wished she was the one biting it instead. "I would very much like to try this."

"If you end up not liking it, it's totally fine," Haley said, resting her hands on the mattress on either side of Vasile. She leaned in, her breath ghosting across the shell of his ear. "But I'd love for you to fuck me with it."

"Haley," Vasile breathed, his voice tight. His grip on the toy tightened and he moaned sharply as her teeth found his earlobe. It was so fun to rile him up. "Just… give me a moment, if you wouldn't mind."

"Take your time. I'll step out for a sec." She tiptoed out into the living room and collected Vasile's coat from the door on her way. It fit her perfectly, save for the arms being just a bit too wide. The fabric was soft against her skin, but heavy and comforting like a weighted blanket. She understood now why he loved it so much.

Haley didn't step into the room again until Vasile announced that he was ready. She pushed the door open shyly, only to be met by a smiling

Vasile, laid out across the bed, vibrant pink dildo between his legs.

And the smile only grew once their eyes met. "I fear I may never be able to take that coat back from you," he said, moving to the edge of the bed and tugging her in by the coat. "It suits you far better than it ever has me."

"That's not true and you know it." Haley moved into his lap, her thighs bracketing his. The phallus pressed against her stomach and his, cold to the touch like the rest of him. She took it into her fist and gave it one slow pump. "How does this feel?"

"Good," Vasile managed. "I like this a lot, despite its... offputting color."

"What, you don't like hot pink?" Haley giggled, quickening her motions on him. Vasile tipped his head back slightly, exposing his long, pale neck. She was starting to get the appeal now. His neck *was* nice. "It won't matter once it's inside of me."

"Haley, *please*," Vasile said, his forehead coming to rest against her chest.

"What do you want?" she asked, carding her fingers through his hair. "Tell me."

He lifted his head, big, pleading eyes meeting hers. "I want to be inside you," he whispered. "God, I want to be inside you more than I have ever wanted anything in my life."

Haley swallowed. Her whole *not getting attached to Vasile* thing was failing. Miserably. If she could see him look upon her with those warm eyes every day, she'd never want for anything else. "Then be inside me," she said. "Put your cock in me, Vasile."

Vasile gripped his cock at its base and Haley raised her hips just enough to position herself over him. She'd had this dildo inside her before, but something about it being connected to Vasile too made it feel better than it ever had.

She gasped against the sudden fullness, her nails digging into the skin of his shoulders. His hands circled her hips as she started to move, tilting her hips to allow the head of his cock to hit the spot inside her that sent bolts of pleasure through her.

"Yes, Haley. You look so good like this," Vasile crooned, his hips snapping up to join hers as she started to move on top of him. "So perfect." His mouth found her neck, fangs grazing the skin. "May I taste you? Just one more time?"

"*Please.*" She couldn't withhold her moan as his teeth sunk into her. It was too much and not enough at the same time–she wanted him to suck her dry, to fuck her until she couldn't see straight. But she was at the end of her rope, the stimulation making her body tremble and her vision swim. The blood being drained from her didn't do much to help that situation. And then his thumb came down to circle her clit and for a split second, she thought she might pass out.

His other hand captured her hip to steady her and she screamed out his name as her orgasm crested inside her. She came around his cock with a shudder and her vision blurred as Vasile pulled his fangs from her. Her blood trickled from the corner of his mouth and his blood-stained tongue darted out to collect it.

And now she thought blood was sexy. This man was single-handedly ruining her.

She didn't dare pull away from him. She wasn't sure she could trust her body to do so. But Vasile's words stopped her in her tracks anyway. "Can we stay here for a little while?" he asked quietly.

Haley nodded, her forehead resting against his shoulder. "I'd like that."

Chapter Nine

Once the aftershocks of their orgasms wore off, they dug Haley's new comforter and pillows out and made themselves comfortable in bed. "As much as I hate to admit a man is ever right," Haley said, tucking herself under Vasile's chin, "you were right about the size of the mattress. I'm glad it's bigger."

"The bed you chose before was entirely too small. You would have hardly fit on it alone." His fingers traced lazy circles on her bare arm, and he dropped a kiss to the top of her head. "At least now you will be comfortable."

"Yeah." She buried her nose into the crook of his neck and breathed in that herbal smell as if to burn it into her nostrils. She was going to miss it.

Haley slid out of bed and pulled her sketchbook and a pencil out of the box that she *really* needed to unpack. She hadn't touched this sketchbook in years, and almost didn't want to think about what could possibly be in it. She flipped to the middle of the book and crawled back into bed.

"What are you doing?" Vasile asked, an amused smile touching his lips.

"Drawing you." She sat cross-legged next to him, facing him, allowing herself to really take in all of his features, all of the little things about him she was going to miss. One of his hands was tucked under his chin, the nearly translucent skin illuminated by the moonlight streaming in through the curtainless window. "What are all those little scars from?" she asked.

Vasile looked down at his hand and splayed it out, tracing the pointer finger of his opposite hand along the tiny, raised bumps. She sketched the outline of his head, the elegant, curved slope of his

Roman nose. "The night that I consumed all of that laudanum… contained many of my worst moments, I am afraid."

Haley's pencil stopped. "I'm sorry, you don't have to talk about it if you don't want to."

"No, I do not mind." His gaze remained trained on his hand. "My turning was still fresh at the time. I had been in the wrong place at the wrong time… I was walking home from work in the dead of night and, the next thing I knew, I was in a dark alley… dying, and then being reborn. I struggled with it for a very long time. The idea of being trapped in a body that was not my own for the rest of eternity felt… like I had been damned.

"I had never tried laudanum in my life before that night. I was sensitive to it, but I did not stop once I lost myself. At one point in the night, I threw my fist into a mirror. Like a child throwing a tantrum." He laughed sadly, the sound not quite reaching his eyes. "I thought creatures like me were not able to see themselves in mirrors. But I did. I saw something that was not myself in more ways than I knew how to handle."

"Vasile," Haley said quietly, reaching for his scarred hand. "I'm sorry, I didn't mean to bring up something so... awful." She smoothed her thumb over the rough skin, and he drew her hand to his mouth and kissed it.

"It is alright. It is part of who I am now." He released her hand and she returned to sketching him, dotting his long, elegant hand with his little scars.

"It makes you look tough. Like a sexy bad boy who got into a bar fight," she teased, and he laughed, the corners of his eyes crinkling. She erased the bright, open eyes she'd just sketched and instead, drew his eyes in cute crescent shapes, laugh lines decorating his eyes and mouth.

This was the version of Vasile she wanted to remember. "I am starting to question your taste in men," he said.

"I get that a lot." She beamed at him and his smile dropped a fraction. His eyes on her were soft, and she swore she saw a slight tremble to his lips in the moonlight.

But he didn't speak. He watched her as she continued to sketch, and she allowed herself to take her time. To appreciate every infuriatingly beautiful angle of his face, the sharp contours of the collarbones that she now knew he *really* liked having kissed. Occasionally, Vasile reached out to rest a hand on her–her ankle, her calf, even moving a bit closer to brush his thumb across her hip bone.

After what felt like approximately ten minutes but must have been hours, the room brightened a little, the sun beginning its climb over the horizon.

"It must be nearly morning already," Vasile murmured. "Have you the time?"

Haley reached blindly behind her for her phone, almost afraid to know the answer. "It's almost five thirty in the morning," she said, tossing her phone back onto the mattress. The sun would be fully risen within the hour, and Vasile would have to sleep. And then, he'd probably be ready to leave her.

"Goodness. The night has gone by so quickly." His hand moved to her head, fingers trailing through her hair. "It feels like an eternity has passed, yet, at the same time... it feels like only an hour."

"I know." She snaked her arms around his torso and pulled him in closer. It was time to rip off the band-aid. "So, you wanna leave tomorrow, huh?"

"Want to? I am unsure. But *need* to?" Vasile sighed. "I have missed so much, Haley. There is so much I wanted to be there for. I am a doctor who is blessed with all the time in the world to discover cures, to invent surgical techniques. I could have learned over the last two centuries and used that knowledge to help people... like me." He swallowed, and Haley immediately felt like the biggest asshole alive. "I do not know what it is like at home anymore. But if a change needs to happen... I have to be part of it."

"I get it," Haley said. And she hated that she did. She couldn't think of a proper argument if she wanted to. "The world still isn't perfect for people like you. Trans people. Even here in America, the country that's supposed to be the 'land of the free' or whatever." She pulled away from Vasile, resting both hands on either side of his face. "I won't hold you back, no matter how much I selfishly kinda want to." She gave a half-hearted laugh, and Vasile's hands came up to cover hers.

"You are an incredibly unselfish person, Haley," he said. "You have done so much for me over the course of a single night. Had anyone else found me... I might not have been so lucky. And I will not be quick to forget that."

But he would. He'd wake up back at home in Romania five, ten, twenty years from now, a wildly successful doctor with someone else on his arm. Another vampire, maybe. Or another human lucky enough to find him. He wouldn't remember the girl with the shitty pick up truck and the empty house.

"I hope you don't." She steeled her jaw against a fresh wave of tears prickling behind her eyelids and kissed him. Her lips wobbled against his, and Vasile removed his hands from hers to pull her into his arms.

"I am not certain there is enough laudanum in the world to make me forget you, Haley," Vasile said.

"I hate to break it to you, but laudanum doesn't exist anymore," Haley muttered, her voice betraying the facade she'd been trying so hard to uphold.

"That is probably for the best." Vasile attempted a laugh, but it came out hollow. Her leg draped over his, anchoring him to her as if it might stop him from ever leaving.

They laid in silence for a few minutes, Haley's finger tracing hearts along the bandages binding Vasile's chest. Vasile's fingers continued through her hair, his nails scratching her scalp. She hadn't slept in well over twenty-four hours now, but there was no way she'd sleep.

She reached for her phone again, searching for flights to Romania. Tickets were expensive, as to be expected with how last minute they were. And she was going to pay for it herself, because her boyfriend-for-a-night had been asleep for two hundred years and didn't have any modern currency.

"I can get you on the way back home at midnight tomorrow," Haley said, trying not to sound quite as defeated as she felt. "Is that okay?"

"Tomorrow at midnight is perfect." Vasile looked like he wanted to say something else. Or maybe it was just wishful thinking.

Was it stupid that she would go with him if he asked? That she would consider uprooting her entire life, selling the house she'd just bought, and moving to a country she'd never been to, just to be with him?

It was stupid to think he would ask her in the first place. No matter what her heart told her, she'd known him for all of eight hours. That was it. He'd go home and they'd move on with their lives.

She ordered his plane ticket and shoved her phone under her pillow. She could pretend for a little while longer.

Chapter Ten

Haley called out of work the next morning to sleep. The last thing she wanted to do was waste what little time she had left with Vasile, but her body didn't give her much of a choice. Vasile fell asleep dutifully as the sun rose, his body wrapped around hers. And she slept on and off, waking only to feed the very confused Brenda. Vasile awoke just after sunset; the sky wasn't pitch black just yet, but the sun was gone just enough to allow him to function.

Haley didn't allow herself to be in bed when Vasile woke. She wasn't sure she could handle waking up next to him, knowing she'd never get to do it again. She showered instead, hoping it would make her feel at least a little more alive.

When she returned to the bedroom after her shower, Vasile was tugging on his clothes, a deep frown creasing his perfect skin. "Everything is so *wrinkled* now," he grumbled under his breath. He had one arm in his coat sleeve when he finally noticed Haley standing in the doorway, a small smile on her lips. "Enjoy your bath?"

"Yeah, it was fine," Haley shrugged. She stepped into the room, helping Vasile with his coat. "How are you feeling?"

"I'm not sure, if I am being honest," he said. Haley untucked his curls from the neck of his coat as he adjusted the ruffles at his sleeves. "Excited, because I miss my home. But...." He looked at Haley, and for a moment, she wondered if this was it, if he was finally going to ask her to come with him. He shook his head. "Everything is frightening, and I do not know what I will do without you."

Haley waved off his concern with a flick of her wrist. "Trust me, you're gonna be totally fine.

You're smart. You'll figure it all out and it'll be like you weren't asleep for two hundred whole years."

Vasile didn't meet her gaze. "I hope you are correct." He did, however, take one of her hands in his, stroking a thumb over the back of it. "Might I ask for a favor before we leave?"

"Sure."

"Could we possibly go back to that restaurant with the... what did you call it? Agua fresca? I would love one of those cinnamon beverages. I am not certain we have them at home."

Haley couldn't say no to him if she tried. "Of course we can. I'll get you the biggest one they have."

Vasile said his goodbyes to Brenda, which hurt Haley more than she thought it would. "Behave yourself, young lady," he said to her, giving her a scratch with one finger under her chin. "Be good to Haley. Take care of her for me."

"Are you a cop?" Brenda chirped, which was the only thing that kept Haley from bursting into tears.

"Say 'bye bye,' Brenda," Haley said, moving next to Vasile to stroke Brenda's head. Brenda simply chirped, rustled her feathers in Vasile's direction, and hopped onto the floor of her cage. Maybe she wasn't ready to say goodbye to him, either.

"Alright, we should probably get going." She started for the door without checking to make sure Vasile was behind her. When she turned around, his back was to her. "You okay?"

"Yes. Just... taking everything in." He returned to her, clasping his coat at his throat. "I am ready."

Well, that made one of them. They got into the truck and Haley took them to the Mexican restaurant first, ordering two of the largest horchatas she could. Vasile looked mildly intimidated by it but sucked away at it happily.

Haley hated that she couldn't bring herself to talk to Vasile for the duration of the drive to the airport. It was only about half an hour from her house, but she knew that if she started talking at all, she'd start crying.

Traffic at the airport was slower tonight; not as many people getting on redeyes meant he'd at least get through security pretty quickly. Which meant he'd be gone faster. Haley pulled up next to the departures door and got out of the car, rounding it to let Vasile out.

"Alright. Do you remember what to do?" she asked.

"Find someone at a desk to speak to about printing my ticket," Vasile said, flicking off the instructions on his fingers, "then find security, then find the gate I am supposed to wait in."

"Exactly." She straightened the lapel of his coat, and before she pulled away, he surprised her by tugging her into his arms. "Vasile–"

"If you ever find yourself in Transylvania, promise you will seek me out," Vasile whispered, his voice thick with tears. "It does not matter what I am doing. I will drop it all to see you."

"What if you're in the middle of a life saving surgery or something?" she muttered into his coat, thoroughly soaking the fabric with her tears.

Vasile laughed shortly. "Perhaps... not including that. But anything else." His hands circled her upper arms as he pulled away. "Take care, Haley. I...."

He stopped, then leaned in to press a feather-light kiss to her lips. "I will miss you."

"I'll miss you, too." Haley didn't let herself be swallowed by her tears until Vasile disappeared into the airport. She shoved the car into drive and pulled away, not allowing herself a second glance.

She didn't get much further than the last departure gate before she pulled over, too blinded by tears to keep driving. There was no point in crying now. He was gone, and now her life would go back to normal, just like it had been before she discovered the stupid box in her basement.

But she didn't *want* normal. She wanted... whatever last night had been. She wanted to sleep tangled in Vasile's arms, to know what it would be like to wake up to his sweet, sleepy face.

She called Rhea, who, as always, answered on the first ring. "Hey, babe, what's up?" Rhea asked, and the sound of her best friend's voice did little more than reduce her to tears again. "Hey, hey. Haley. Talk to me."

Haley sniffled, forcing a quivering breath into her lungs. "I didn't want him to leave," she managed. "I just dropped him off at the airport and I wish I was going with him. Is that stupid? Am I being stupid?"

Rhea let out a long sigh that crackled in Haley's ear. "Yes, it is. Incredibly so. You've known this guy for, what, two days?"

"Not even two days," Haley grumbled, wiping her eyes with the heel of her palm. "Rhea... what if he's the one? What if he's *it* and I just let him fly across the world and I never see him again?"

Rhea was silent for a beat. "It sounds like you already know what you wanna do."

She did. She'd known what she wanted to do since she'd found him in her living room, Brenda perched on the crook of his finger. "It's stupid," she said. "I shouldn't want to follow a guy across the world, right?"

"Want and need are two very different things," Rhea said.

And Haley *knew* the difference. "If I park my car in the parking lot here, will you come get it for me?"

"Of course I will," Rhea said. Haley slammed the car into drive and peeled away from the departures gate, circling the airport to find the parking garage. Luckily, it was probably going to take Vasile a hell of a long time to get through the airport. She had no doubt in her mind he'd managed to get lost. "I'll stay with Brenda for as long as I can."

"You're a saint, thank you." Haley pulled into the first parking space she found and leaped out of her truck. "Thank you for never making me feel crazy."

"Oh, you *are* crazy," Rhea said, and Haley could hear the grin in her voice. "And I love you for it. Go get your man."

Haley didn't have to be told twice. She took off running through the parking garage and into the airport, her worn sneakers slipping on the tile beneath her. The airport was rather quiet at this time of night, which she hoped would make it easy to find Vasile. The flight left in half an hour, but maybe, if she was lucky, he'd gotten himself delayed somewhere.

She got as close to the security checkpoint as she could without a ticket and there he was, squinting against the airport's oppressively bright lighting in the middle of the security line. "Vasile!" she shouted, cupping her hands over her mouth. His head whipped around to her, mouth dropping open in surprise.

"Haley!"

She shoved her way through the security line, earning her a few grunts and shouts of irritation. But she didn't care. The only thing in this entire airport, in this entire fucking city, that mattered was Vasile.

She flung herself into his arms once she reached him, burying her face in his neck. He caught her, arms wrapping around her middle. "What are you doing here?" Vasile asked softly, stroking a hand over her still-damp hair.

Haley pulled back, capturing his face in both of her hands. "I'm gonna say something really crazy and... you can respond however you want. You can tell me I'm crazy and to fuck off and I'd be fine with that. I really hope you don't, but I could be fine with it." Vasile's brow furrowed. "I moved to New York for a new start... to find some meaning to my life. I wanted to find inspiration. I wanted to start painting again. I stopped painting years ago and I lost myself. I didn't know who I was anymore.

"But now here *you* are, this... beautiful, kind, smart man who waltzed into my life, flipped it upside down, then left the next day." Haley laughed, smoothing her thumbs over his cheekbones. "My inspiration came back. I forgot what it felt like to see beauty in every day moments, but God, when you're there, every moment feels like I'm living in Monet's fucking *Artist's Garden.*"

Vasile's eyes shimmered with tears, and Haley could practically feel every eye in the airport boring into the side of her head. But she didn't care. "I don't wanna be here without you, Vasile. I wanna be with you."

"Haley...." His jaw visibly tightened, and for a brief moment, Haley thought maybe he *was* going to tell her to fuck off. "I was so frightened to ask you to come with me. I could not ask you to leave your home, the house you have only just bought.

You have a life, and I happened to stumble upon it. You did not ask for my intrusion." He took both of her hands in hers. "But I could not have wished for anything more. You have left a permanent mark on me, Haley. I will most assuredly never be the same now that you have touched my life, even for a passing moment." Haley let out a laugh mixed with a sob, and Vasile took the liberty of wiping the tears from her cheeks. "I would be most honored if you wished to come with me, though I would never dream of forcing you to."

"You should've just asked me, dummy. Then we could've avoided this whole thing," Haley teased weakly, drawing their joined hands to her lips. She brushed her lips across his knuckles. "So we're doing this? Together?"

"For as long as you shall have me," Vasile whispered, then drew her in for a long, searing kiss. The other passengers erupted into cheers, and Haley found herself grinning against Vasile's lips. This was among the stupider things she'd ever done in her life, but also, she wasn't sure she'd change it for the world.

Epilogue

"Okay, babe, hold still. This might hurt a little."

Vasile winced, despite the fact that the needle was still *far* from his thigh. "I am a doctor. I know what a needle feels like," he said, and Haley gave his cheek an affectionate pinch. She caught his chin between her thumb and forefinger and kissed him, plunging the needle into his thigh at the same time. "Did you just give me a shot without watching what you were doing?" he all but squealed.

"Yep. It worked, didn't it?" She capped the needle and tossed it into the sharps container Vasile had so dutifully bought to live in their bathroom. "First shot, baby. How does it feel?"

"Like I still cannot believe it is something we are capable of doing," he said, rubbing at the injection site once Haley covered it with a band-aid. "It does not feel real quite yet."

"It will, once you grow lots of sexy chest hair and a beard." She straddled his waist and he rested his hands on her hips. "You'd look hot with a beard."

Vasile stroked his chin thoughtfully. "A beard sounds... exhausting. Would the stubble not irritate your skin?"

"Nah. I'd like it." As if to prove her point, she peppered kisses along his jawline, his grip on her tightening. "But you're plenty hot without a beard, don't worry."

"What a relief," Vasile said sarcastically, and Haley grinned. "You are also quite ravishing without a beard."

"Damn. I was thinking about growing one." She gave him a quick peck on the lips before standing up. "Rhea should be here any minute... but I think we have a little time." She rested her hands on his bare knees, coming face-to-face with him. "You wanna take this party to the bedroom?"

Vasile laughed, leaning forward to kiss her. "Perhaps it is the testosterone raging through my body... but right now, I need nothing more than to take my beautiful girl to bed."

Haley lifted a dramatic hand to her forehead and fell into Vasile. "Oh, my big, strong man, I need you to carry me to bed! My feeble little lady legs won't carry me!"

"As you wish, fair maiden." He scooped her into his arms and stood which, to be fair, he'd been able to do from the moment she met him. But she never got tired of it. He walked her from the bathroom into their bedroom, laying her out on their massive bed. Sometimes, she thought their bed was *too* big.

"Come here," Haley purred, dragging Vasile to her level by his collar. He'd taken to wearing slightly more modern clothing now, no matter how much he complained about it. But every now and then, she *really* missed that ruffled collar. *And* the coat. He crawled on top of her and kissed her neck, fangs poised to sink in when a knock sounded at the door.

Of fucking course. Haley was delighted to see Rhea, but that didn't mean she had to be entirely grateful for the cock block. "We'll pick this up later," she promised, nipping at his throat with her own blunt teeth before rolling out of bed from under him.

Haley opened the door and Rhea spread her arms wide to allow Haley to immediately leap into them. "My baby!" Rhea laughed, spinning Haley in a circle. "God, I missed your stupid face. Look at you! You are absolutely glowing!"

Haley rested her hands on her cheeks. "Yeah, you'd be surprised at the amount of color you get in your face when you actually go outside." Her schedule had become nocturnal, for the most part. But the new setting had delivered some much-needed inspiration, and she found herself sneaking out in the middle of the day to paint.

Which she hadn't done in years. She hadn't gained her speed back yet; her last painting had taken her the entirety of the six months they'd been in Romania. And it hung above their mantle, Vasile's gentle, kind face peering down at them.

Rhea peeked into the house. "So? Where is he?" she asked, and Haley laughed, tugging her inside.

"Vasile! Rhea's here!" She shut the door behind Rhea so as not to let the last rays of sunset into the house. "I can't believe you're here!"

"Me either. This was a hell of a flight," Rhea said. This was the longest Haley had ever gone without seeing Rhea, and she suddenly wondered how she'd made it so long. She'd cut her hair short again, sporting a blunt bob that Haley didn't think looked good on anyone but Rhea. Her hair was black again after a solid few years of blue. It suited her.

"Bitch!" came a squawk from the corner of the living room.

Rhea whipped around on her heel, narrowing her eyes. "Y'know, you'd think Brenda would learn to be appreciative of me after I personally made sure she was reunited with her mother who moved halfway across the world." She let out a little gasp. "Wait, who's this beautiful angel?"

"That is Myrtle," came Vasile's voice. He approached the cage and offered his finger to the green-feathered budgie who now shared her cage with Brenda. Brenda hadn't been entirely happy about her new roommate at first, but a few weeks ago, Haley had caught her preening Myrtle's feathers. So they were getting somewhere.

Myrtle hopped onto Vasile's finger and chirped, and Rhea smoothed a finger over her little head. "She's so cute," Rhea grinned. "*Way* cuter than Brenda." Haley would let it slide this time. Rhea had earned the right to be mean to Brenda, just this once. Rhea turned her attention to Vasile. "So, you're the famous Vasile that my best friend fled the country for."

Vasile's face paled, and Haley clicked her tongue. "Dude. Seriously?" Myrtle hopped back into her cage and Haley came over to close it. "Be nice."

"I *am* being nice! It's not like I'm lying!" Rhea folded her arms, staring pointedly at Vasile. "So why didn't you ask her to come back to Romania with you when you left?"

Vasile blanched before carefully rearranging his face. "I did not want to uproot her life simply so that I could be near her. I had my own goals and she had hers. It is not my place to demand anything of her."

Rhea pursed her lips as if deciding if the answer was good enough. She had always been like this, though maybe not always to this extent. But then again, Haley had never moved to a different country for a guy, either. "And how likely is it for you to take so many drugs you end up asleep for two hundred years again?"

At the same time as Haley whined "Rhea!" Vasile actually laughed. "Unlikely. Very much so. I was at a different point in my life back then. A very sad one. But I have Haley now... and I cannot imagine feeling sad even for a moment." He cast those big, warm eyes in her direction, and she felt as if she was going to melt into a puddle at his feet. She hugged him around the middle, and he dropped a kiss to the top of her head.

Rhea's nose wrinkled. "Fine, fine, you two are sickeningly in love. I get it." Haley unraveled herself from around Vasile to take Rhea's outstretched hand. "I'm stealing Haley away for a little bit. For some best friend time. Is that okay?"

Haley *knew* this was a test, and Vasile passed it with flying colors. "Of course. Take all the time you need."

They left the house and started down the lawn towards the pond. The ducks were out in full force, a few napping by the side of the water, a few leisurely paddling through the pond. "It's even cuter than the pictures made it look," Rhea grinned, taking a seat cross-legged just far enough away from the pond so as not to be a disturbance to the ducks. "So... Vasile's sweet. And you're right, he *is* pretty hot."

"I know, right?" Haley pulled her knees to her chest and rested her chin on them. "I thought moving in with him was crazy. We got here and I was like... 'holy shit, I'm in a different country with a guy I've known for a *day*.'" She turned her face towards Rhea, her cheek mashed against her knee.

"But he's amazing. He's teaching me Romanian, he brings me breakfast when he comes home from work every morning, after spending all night delivering gender affirming care to trans people. And on top of all that... he's *amazing* in bed."

"God, I hate you so much," Rhea said and Haley laughed, giving her shoulder a shove. "Your dream man literally fell into your lap."

"It'll happen for you, too. You just need to stay off those dating apps."

Rhea scoffed. "The dating apps are useless anyway. I swear, they attract the worst people. I went on a date with this girl yesterday and she said she loved me *on the date.* And then she DM'd me afterwards, saying her ex wanted to get back with her so she didn't wanna go on another date."

"Yikes," Haley grimaced.

Rhea shrugged, picking at a loose thread on the sleeve of her sweater. "It's fine. It'll come to me one day, and then maybe they'll love me so much, they'll want a portrait of my face in our living room, too." She knocked her knee against Haley's.

"I took the painting home. It's not in *my* living room, but... it *is* in my bedroom."

Haley had finally texted Rhea about the portrait when she went to the house to pick up Brenda. She hadn't brought many of her belongings over to Romania with her, so giving Rhea the portrait she'd been hanging onto for years felt... right. It was finally time for her to see it.

"I'm really glad you like it," Haley said, her head coming to rest against Rhea's shoulder. "I'll do a better one soon, I promise."

"No, it's perfect." Rhea wrapped an arm around Haley, tugging her closer. "I love you so much."

Haley smiled. "I love you, too."

Acknowledgements

I can't believe I'm writing the acknowledgements for my third book—this feels so incredibly surreal. My publishing journey has been such a wonderful, exciting one filled with the kindest people I've ever met, and I'm so lucky to be part of this community.

Thank you, first and foremost, to everyone who has read this in all its messy stages: Ash, Quin, Claire, Theo, and Duckie. All of your feedback made this novella what it is, and I couldn't be happier with how it turned out.

Extra special thanks to Duckie, one of my biggest cheerleaders and general sweetest human being alive. Thank you for always being willing to leave silly, unhinged comments on my writing when I need it most. I'm so lucky to know you.

And as always, thanks to Ash, the better half of my heart, my cover designer, my biggest inspiration and cheerleader. Thank you for loving me. It's because of you that I can write characters like Vasile, characters that are so incredibly personal to me that deserve the kind of love you give me every day.

And thank YOU, for reading this book! If you feel so inclined, please do leave a review on Goodreads, Amazon, Storygraph, or wherever suits your fancy!

About the Author

KC De la Rosa (he/him) is an author of alien and monster romance that is always queer and sometimes spicy. Sometimes he writes messy rom-com level romances, sometimes he writes high-octane sci-fi romances about bounty hunters. But you can always count on there being a happily ever after. He lives in Georgia with his author spouse and two dogs, Chai and Milkshake.

www.ingramcontent.com/pod-product-compliance
Lightning Source LLC
Chambersburg PA
CBHW062214150726
47991CB00006B/2280